Tom and Ricky

and

A Voice in the Night

Bob Wright

High Noon Books
Novato, California

Cover Design: Nancy Peach
Interior Illustrations: Herb Heidinger

Glossary: planet, child, dream, crow, parrot, captain

International Standard Book Number: 0-87879-362-3

9 8 7 6 5 4
5 4 3 2 1 0 9 8

Contents

CHAPTER 1

A Bad Dream

Tom, Ricky, and Eddie started to walk home. They had just seen the new space movie.

"I liked that movie," Eddie said.

"I liked the part where the star ships went to the yellow planet," Tom said.

"Me, too," Ricky said.

"Boy, it was good. I want to see it again," Eddie said.

"How many hot dogs did you have?" Tom asked.

"Three," Eddie said.

"And three bags of popcorn," Ricky said.

"I didn't eat all of it. You and Tom kept on eating it," Eddie said.

"We had just a little," Tom said.

"You know what? I don't feel very well," Eddie said.

"I can see why," Ricky said.

"When I eat too much at the movies, I have bad dreams," Eddie said.

"I'll bet you have some tonight," Ricky said.

"Well, here we are. Home at last," Eddie said.

"Do you want to do anything tomorrow?" Tom asked.

"OK. Maybe we can all go to the Video Store," Eddie said.

"They have a new game down there," Tom said.

"Or we could go fishing," Ricky said.

"We will call you. Take care," Tom said.

Tom and Ricky started to walk to their homes. Eddie went into his house.

"Did he really have three hot dogs?" Tom asked.

"He sure did. I can see why he might have a bad dream," Ricky said.

Eddie went to his room. He got ready for bed. He put the light out and got into bed. It was dark.

"I should not have had all that food," Eddie said to himself.

Soon Eddie fell asleep.

The child was lost in the woods. Eddie could hear the small child cry.

4

He started to dream. In his dream he saw a small child. The child was lost in the woods. Eddie could hear the small child cry.

The child was calling, "Take me home. Take me home. Please take me home."

In his dream, Eddie called back, "I will help you. I will help you. Stay where you are."

In his dream Eddie ran and looked for the small child. But he couldn't find anyone.

The child was crying, "Take me home. Take me home. Please help me."

In his dream Eddie ran and ran. He bumped into a tree. Then he woke up.

He was out of bed. He had bumped into the door. That's what woke him up.

"What a dream!" Eddie said to himself. He put on the light. No one was in the room.

"Why did I eat all those hot dogs and all that popcorn? Well, it was just a dream," he said. He put out the light and went back to bed.

It was very dark. "I'm glad that dream is over," he thought to himself.

But the dream wasn't over. It started up again.

The small child called out again. "Take me home. Take me home. Please take me home." The child's voice seemed very close.

Eddie thought to himself, "I'm not sleeping. I'm awake. You can't have a dream when you are awake!" He sat up in his bed.

Then the lost child said a very funny thing.

The lost child called out, "It's your turn to do the dishes."

"What's going on?" Eddie said.

CHAPTER 2

Cookies

Tom and Ricky went over to Eddie's house the next day. They waited in front.

"He said he'd be ready," Tom said.

"You know Eddie. He's slow," Ricky said.

"Let's call him," Tom said.

"Eddie! Eddie! Come on out," Ricky called.

Eddie looked out. "I'm not up yet. Come on in."

Tom and Ricky went in the house.

"Aren't you ready yet?" Tom asked.

"I didn't sleep well last night," Eddie said.

"I can see why. You ate too much at the movie," Tom said.

"Maybe I did," Eddie said.

"You mean you didn't sleep at all?" Ricky asked.

"Well, I did just a little," Eddie said.

"How do you feel now?" Tom asked.

"I feel OK now," Eddie said.

"Well, then let's get going," Ricky said.

"You know what?" Eddie said.

"No, what?" Tom answered.

"I had a bad dream. I had it over and over again. But it didn't seem like a dream. I'm sure I was awake," Eddie answered.

"What kind of a dream was it?" Ricky asked.

"It was about a small child who was lost in the woods," Eddie said.

"Why was that a bad dream?" Tom asked.

"I tried to find the child. But I couldn't," Eddie answered.

"Was it a boy or a girl?" Ricky asked.

"I don't know. I never saw the little kid," Eddie answered.

"Well, how do you know it was a small child?" Tom asked.

"I could tell from the voice," Eddie said.

"What did the kid say? The kid must have said something," Ricky said.

"The kid said, 'Take me home. Take me home. Please take me home.' The kid said that over and over again."

"Was the voice far away?" Tom asked.

"No. It was like it was right outside the house," Eddie said.

"It was just a dream, Eddie," Ricky said.

"It sure seemed real to me," Eddie answered.

"Did the kid just ask to go home? Is that all the kid said?" Tom asked.

"No. And this is funny," Eddie said.

"What's funny?" Ricky asked.

"Right at the end of all the dreams the kid said, 'It's your turn to do the dishes.' Now how about that?" Eddie said.

Tom and Ricky started to laugh. Eddie laughed, too.

"I think I did have too much popcorn last night," Eddie said.

"You know what?" Tom said.

"What?" Ricky asked.

"Dave told me he had a bad dream. And there was a lost child in his dream, too," Tom said.

"Did Dave say the kid said anything?" Eddie asked.

"The small child said he wanted to go home," Tom said.

"Was there anything about doing the dishes?" Eddie asked.

"Well, this is really funny," Tom said.

"What's that?" Ricky asked.

"The kid kept saying 'Who has the cookies?'"

CHAPTER 3

More Dreams

Eddie was getting ready to go. Tom and Ricky sat. They wanted him to hurry up.

"Where shall we go?" Ricky asked.

"How about going to the creek today?" Tom said.

"That's a good idea. I can play that new video game some other time," Eddie said.

They all got on their bikes. They went down Front Street. That was the fast way to get to the creek.

"Look. Is that Dave?" Eddie called out.

"It sure is," Tom called back.

"Who is he talking to?" Eddie asked.

"Look. Is that Dave?"

Dave was next to a police car.

"That's Sergeant Collins," Ricky said.

The three boys stopped next to the car.

"Where are you going?" Dave called out.

"Down to the creek," Eddie answered.

"How's everything?" Sergeant Collins said to his friends.

"Fine," Tom said.

"How about you?" Ricky asked Sergeant Collins.

"We were just talking about dreams," the Sergeant said.

"Dreams?" Eddie asked.

"That's what we've been talking about," Ricky said.

"Everyone is talking about dreams," Dave said.

"What do you mean?" Ricky asked.

"I was telling Sergeant Collins about my dream. I had the same one for two nights. There was this kid in my dream. Then my mom had the same dream," Dave said.

"The same dream?" Tom asked.

"That's not all. Then my dad had the same dream," Dave said.

"So did I," Eddie said.

Ricky looked at Sergeant Collins. "Can everyone have the same dream?"

Tom looked at Sergeant Collins, too. "How about it?" he said.

"I don't know. I don't know anything about dreams. But I've never heard of so many people having the same dream," he answered.

"Maybe it isn't a dream. Maybe there really is a lost child," Ricky said.

"Well, I sure would know about it," the Sergeant said.

"What are you working on now?" Tom asked.

"Someone took a car. Some money is missing at the bank. Someone broke into Mr. Green's pet store," he answered.

"You have a lot to do," Ricky said.

"I sure do. I'll be seeing all of you. I have to go," the Sergeant said.

Sergeant Collins took off in his car.

"You know. Maybe this isn't a dream at all," Ricky said.

"What do you mean," Eddie asked.

"I think Sergeant Collins is right. How could so many people have the same dream?" Ricky asked.

"What can we do about it?" Dave asked.

"Let's all stay at Eddie's house tonight. We'll all see if we hear the child's voice. Then we can clear up this mystery," Ricky said.

CHAPTER 4

The Next Move

It was night. Tom, Ricky, and Dave were all at Eddie's house. They were going to find out more about the bad dream everyone was having.

"Did you have any hot dogs today?" Ricky asked Eddie.

"No way," Eddie said.

"Where are the cookies your mom gave us?" Tom asked Eddie.

"By my bed," Eddie answered.

"Let me have one more," Tom said.

"OK. Is everyone ready?" Eddie asked.

"Ready as we'll ever be," Ricky said.

Eddie got in his bed.

Ricky jumped up. "Get the lights on. I heard the small child!"

Tom, Ricky, and Dave were on the floor.

"Lights out," Tom called.

Eddie turned the lights out. No one said anything. It was a dark night.

All of a sudden they heard a voice say, "Move your leg."

Ricky jumped up. "Get the lights on. I heard the small child!"

Eddie turned the lights on. "What's up?" he asked.

"I heard the small child say 'Move your leg,'" Ricky said.

"That was me. I was telling Dave to move his leg," Tom said.

"OK. Ready? Lights out," Ricky said.

Eddie turned the lights out. Again it was dark.

Then someone said, "Who has the cookies?"

Ricky said, "They're right by Eddie."

Again, someone said, "Who has the cookies?"

"I told you they are by Eddie. I'll get them," Ricky said. He put his hand by Eddie's bed and got the cookies.

"Here," he said.

No one said anything.

"Here are the cookies," Ricky said again.

"What's going on?" Eddie called out.

"Tom wants the cookies," Ricky said.

"I don't want the cookies," Tom said.

"But you asked for them," Ricky said.

"It wasn't me. I thought it was Dave," Tom said.

"It wasn't me," Dave said.

Eddie sat up in bed. "That's it. That's the child's voice!" Eddie turned on the light.

"What's going on?" Tom asked.

"We heard it. We heard the small child," Ricky said.

"The child?" Tom asked.

They all jumped up.

"Come on. The child must be near here," Ricky said.

"OK. Let's all go out. Let's see if we can find the kid," Eddie said.

24

CHAPTER 5

Nothing

Tom, Ricky, Eddie, and Dave looked all over. They didn't hear the voice in the dark. They didn't see anything.

"Let's all go back in," Eddie called out.

"That's fine with me. I'm cold," Tom said.

They all went back into Eddie's room.

"Did anyone see anything? Did anyone hear anything?" Ricky asked.

"I heard a dog barking," Tom said.

"Maybe it was Patches," Eddie said.

"Did anyone see anything?" Ricky asked.

"I did," Dave said.

They all looked at him.

"No. I saw a big, fat crow up on a pole.

"Did you see the small child?" Eddie asked.

"No. I saw a big, fat crow up on a pole," Dave said.

"A crow?" Ricky asked.

"Yes. It was just sitting on the pole," Dave said.

They all looked out into Eddie's yard. "Well, I don't see it. Does anyone see it?"

"Well, that wasn't much help. A crow isn't a lost child," Tom said.

"It's late. Let's get some sleep," Eddie said.

"If anyone hears the child, say something," Tom said.

"We can all go and see Sergeant Collins in the morning," Ricky said.

"We can tell him that the lost child isn't a dream," Tom said.

"If it isn't a dream, what is it?" Ricky said.

"That's right. We all heard the child ask for the cookies," Eddie said.

"We all looked for the kid," Ricky said.

"And we didn't see anything," Tom said.

"But the voice was so close. It was like it was in the room," Eddie said.

"Well, we did try to find the kid," Ricky said.

"And we know now this isn't a bad dream," Eddie said.

CHAPTER 6

Sergeant Collins

It was morning. Tom, Ricky, Eddie, and Dave all woke up at the same time.

"Come on. We've got to see Sergeant Collins," Eddie said.

Dave looked out into the yard.

"What are you doing?" Tom asked.

"I wanted to see if that big, fat crow was still on the pole," Dave answered.

"Is he?" Tom asked.

"No," Dave answered.

"OK. I'm ready. How about the rest of you?" Ricky asked.

They all went out and got on their bikes. They went right down to see Sergeant Collins.

"Hello, all of you. You came at a good time," Sergeant Collins said.

"Did you find the missing child?" Ricky asked.

"No. But I cleared up all the other things," he said.

"You mean you found the missing car?" Eddie asked.

"Yes. I found the missing car. I got the men who took the money from the bank," Sergeant Collins said.

30

"What about the pet store?" Ricky asked.

"We still don't know who broke into Mr. Green's pet store," Sergeant Collins said.

"Did they take anything?" Eddie asked.

"Mr. Green didn't have much money there. So, they broke some things. They let some of the animals and birds get away," Sergeant Collins said.

"Has Mr. Green found his animals yet?" Ricky asked.

"He has found most of them. But some are still missing," Sergeant Collins answered.

"I wish we could help Mr. Green. But we're still looking for the lost child. We just can't seem to find that kid," Ricky said.

"What have you found out?" Sergeant Collins asked.

"We stayed at Eddie's last night," Tom said.

"Did you see the kid?" Sergeant Collins asked.

"No, but we did hear him," Eddie said.

"What did he say?" Sergeant Collins asked.

"He asked for the cookies. Maybe he wanted some food," Ricky said.

"There's something funny going on," the Sergeant said.

"Can you help us?" Ricky asked.

"I don't have much to go on," Sergeant Collins said.

"We'll keep on looking," Ricky said.

"Good luck. Let me know if you find out anything," the Sergeant said.

"We sure will," Ricky called to him.

The boys got back to their bikes.

"Now what do we do?" Eddie said.

"Let's stop and see Mr. Green. Maybe we can help him," Ricky said.

They all started for Mr. Green's pet store.

CHAPTER 7

A Good Idea

Mr. Green's pet store wasn't far away. They got there very fast. When they got there, Mr. Green was cleaning his store. He seemed to have a lot to do.

"Hi, Mr. Green," Ricky said.

"Hello to all of you. What can I do for you?" he asked.

"We just saw Sergeant Collins. He told us about the missing animals. Can we help you?" Ricky asked.

"My store is open again. I found most of the animals. I just need to find one more," Mr. Green said.

"Where were all the animals?" Eddie asked.

"They all stayed near the store. I found them right away," Mr. Green said.

"Which one is still missing?" Ricky asked.

"Captain Kidd," Mr. Green said.

"Captain Kidd?" Tom said.

"Yes, Captain Kidd is a parrot. He's old. He can't go very far. He has to be near the store," Mr. Green said.

"I bet you miss him," Dave said.

"I sure do. I've had him for a long time," Mr. Green said.

"Do you think he will come back?" Eddie asked.

"I hope so. He is like a child to me," Mr. Green said.

"Another missing child," Eddie said.

"Where do you think he might go?" Dave asked.

"I think he must be near here. He's old. He can't fly very well. He likes to sit up on poles. That way he can see what is going on," Mr. Green said.

"We're looking for a lost child. We might as well look for a lost parrot," Eddie said.

The boys started to go out of the store. Then Ricky turned back. "Wait!" he said.

"What is it?" Mr. Green asked.

"Can parrots really say things?" Ricky asked.

"Sure they can. They can't say much. But they can say things over and over," Mr. Green said.

"Does Captain Kidd talk?" Ricky asked.

"Parrots don't really talk. But Captain Kidd can say some things," Mr. Green answered.

Ricky and Tom looked at each other. They started to laugh.

"What's so funny?" Eddie asked.

"Why are you laughing?" Dave asked.

CHAPTER 8

The Mystery is Cleared Up

Tom and Ricky couldn't stop laughing. Eddie, Dave, and Mr. Green were looking at them. They didn't know what was so funny.

"What's so funny?" Eddie asked.

"Let us in on it," Dave said.

"What's going on?" Eddie asked.

Mr. Green didn't know what to say.

"You'll see," Tom said.

Then Ricky asked Mr. Green, "Does Captain Kidd like cookies?"

"Why, he sure does. He asks for them all the time."

"Does Captain Kidd always ask to go home?" Ricky asked.

"Yes, he does. How did you know that?" Mr Green asked.

Then Eddie asked, "Mr. Green, does Captain Kidd ever say, 'It's your turn to do the dishes'?"

"Why, yes he does. How did you know that? What's going on?" Mr. Green asked.

"I think we've found the lost child," Ricky said.

"The lost child?" Dave asked.

"What do you mean?" Mr. Green asked.

Ricky told Mr. Green about the bad dreams people were having. He told him what people heard in their dreams.

"Do you think it was Captain Kidd?" Mr. Green asked.

"We think so," Ricky said.

"How do you know?" Mr. Green asked.

"Dave saw a crow sitting on a pole. But it was dark. In the dark Captain Kidd would look like a fat crow," Ricky said.

"But a parrot doesn't look like a crow," Mr. Green said.

"But it was dark," Ricky said.

"I think that maybe Captain Kidd might be near Eddie's house," Mr. Green said.

"Come on. Let's go there, " Ricky said.

Tom, Ricky, Eddie, and Dave got there first. Then Mr. Green got there in his car.

All of a sudden a bright, red and green parrot landed on Mr. Green's arm.

"We'll soon find out if you saw a crow or Captain Kidd," Mr. Green said.

Mr. Green took a cookie out of his coat. "Who has all the cookies?" he called out.

All of a sudden a bright, red and green parrot landed on Mr. Green's arm.

"Here's your cookie, Captain Kidd," Mr. Green said.

Then Captain Kidd said, "Take me home. Take me home. Please take me home."

"I will, Captain Kidd. I will," Mr. Green said.

That clears up that mystery," Ricky said.

Mr. Green started to go. "You boys come by and see me soon, will you?"

"We sure will," Ricky answered.

Then Eddie said, "You know what? I feel like having a hot dog and some popcorn."

"A hot dog and some popcorn?" Ricky said.

"Look! That crow is back up there on that pole," Dave called out.

"Come on. Let's all ride down to the creek," Ricky said.

Tom looked back up at the crow. "I hope he doesn't come down and ask for a cookie!"